An extract
D0345729
By Tom Ellen
THE CARTOONS THAT CAME TO LIFE
Illustrated by
Phil Corbett
Chicken House
2 PALMER STREET, FROME,
SOMERSET BA11 1DS

This extract is taken from *The Cartoons That Came to Life* by Tom Ellen, illustrated by Phil Corbett

First published in Great Britain in 2021
Chicken House
2 Palmer Street
Frome, Somerset BA11 1DS
United Kingdom
www.chickenhousebooks.com

Designed and typeset by Steve Wells

British Library Cataloguing in Publication data available.

PB ISBN 978-1-910002-88-9
eISBN 978-1-913322-42-7

3.07 p.m. on a drizzly Thursday …

ARLEY & TAPPER VS PROFESSOR FART-MUNCH
BY FINN MORRIS
LA DI DA I ♡ MY JOB AS A BUS DRIVER FOR THE ADORABLE KITTEN SANCTUARY
NEARLY HOME NOW KITTENS
ST MEREDITH'S TINY ADORABLE KITTEN SANCTUARY FOR TINY ADORABLE KITTENS
BUT THEN...
WAAAHHH A BOULDER!
MEW!
BOUNCE
BOUNCE
CRASH!

OH NO THAT BUS FULL OF ADORABLE KITTENS IS HANGING PERILOUSLY OVER THE BRIDGE
WHO COULD HAVE DONE SUCH A THING?
IT WAS I PROFESSOR FART-MUNC THE EVIL-EST, SMELLY-BOTTOMEST VILLAIN EVER!
WITH JUST ONE PUSH THESE DELIGHTFUL FELINES WILL PLUMMET TO THEIR DOOM MWAHAHAHAHAHA!
TAP TAP
NOT SO FAST MATEY CHOPS!
ARLEY AND TAPPER ??!!
THAT'S RIGHT FART-MUNCH
WE'RE HERE TO SAVE THE DAY AGAIN
YEAH, WE'RE HERE TO DAVE THE SAY AGAIN... WAIT... NO... HANG ON...
SIGH

LET ME DO THE TALKING TAPPER
RIGHT-O ARL!
MEDDLESOME FOOLS
PREPARE TO MEET YOUR DOOM!
OH MONKEY NUTS! WHAT ARE WE GOING TO DO?
TIME FOR OUR SPECIAL MOVES, TAPS,
THE TAIL SPIN!
AND THE SNOT SHOT!
SNIFF!
SNIFF!
TAIL WHIZZ
WOOOSSHHHHH!
UGH! THIS IS DISGUSTING

I GUESS HE NOSE NOT TO MESS WITH US, NOW, ARL?!
DO YOU GET IT?
COS I USED MY
SAVE THE WISE-CRACKS FOR LATER
NOSE
WE'VE GOT KITTENS TO SAVE!
GRAB IT!
HELP US!
THE BUS IS SLIPPING!
READY, TAPS? AFTER 3 WE PULL IT UP TOGETHER
1
2
3

CHAPTER ONE

DAYDREAMING AND DOODLING

'Finn Morris . . . Daydreaming and doodling again, are we?' My maths teacher, Mrs Orlick, is standing over me, her fingers tapping the comic strip I'm drawing.

I blink and look up. Ten seconds ago, I was lost in my own cartoon fantasy world. And now I'm right back in maths at 3.07 p.m. on a drizzly Thursday.

Arley →

Oh, **MONKEY NUTS.**

'Dearie me, Finn,' Mrs Orlick sighs. 'You ALWAYS seem to have your head in the clouds, don't you?'

People start giggling and I can feel myself going red. It's not like I MEANT for this to happen. I honestly didn't.

I started this maths lesson the same way I start EVERY maths lesson – by telling myself: 'I WILL focus this time. I WILL listen to what boring old Mrs Orlick is drooooooning on about.' But the problem is, as soon as Mrs Orlick opens her mouth, ideas for cartoons start flooding into my brain. And they're always WAY more interesting than school.

See, I've wanted to be a cartoonist since . . . well, for ever. I love drawing cartoons of anything – cars, birds, my bad cat Milligan. You name it, I'll cartoonify it.

But what I REALLY love drawing is **ARLEY & TAPPER**! Because unlike

← Tapper

cars, birds and my bad cat Milligan, Arley and Tapper are my creations. I made them up, all on my own.

Mrs Orlick gives me a crinkly smile. 'You've only been at this school two months, Finn, but this must be the TENTH time I've caught you drawing cartoons when you SHOULD be working.'

There's a snuffly SNORT of laughter, and I know without even looking that it came from the nose of Barney Divney. You'd probably recognize him if you saw him, because I've made him the baddie in my **ARLEY & TAPPER** cartoons – the evil **PROFESSOR FART-MUNCH**!

Just like Fart-Munch, Barney's a big, blonde, windy-bottomed BULLY. He stomps around school with his two super-awful sidekicks, Gus and Dolly, using anyone smaller than him as a punch bag.

Mrs Orlick picks up my sketchbook and squints at it through her ridonkulously thick glasses.

What do we have here?
'Arley and Tapper'

The whole class is laughing now, and my face is bright TOMATO red. Everyone is staring at me. Well, nearly everyone. A girl called Isha Kapesa – who I've never spoken to, but who has an AWESOME Marvel Avengers pencil case – is just looking blankly out of the window. I feel weirdly grateful to her.

Mrs Orlick squints harder at my cartoon. 'And who's this . . . ?' she says. '"**PROFESSOR FART-MUNCH**"?'

OH, MONKEY NUTS.

She turns to Barney. 'Why, Barney . . . he looks rather like YOU!'

OH, FAMILY-SIZED BAG OF MONKEY NUTS.

The whole class goes quiet. No one would

ever DARE laugh at Barney Divney.

Barney is glaring at me like he wants to do keepy-uppies with my tonsils.

'Anyway,' Mrs Orlick says. 'That's enough daydreaming and doodling. Let's get back to our six times tables, shall we?'

She walks back to the whiteboard, and Barney gives me a horrid scowl.

'I'M GONNA GET *YOU*, FINN MORRIS!' he whispers.

CHAPTER TWO

SUPER-DUPER UN-SWEET

When the bell rings, I wait till Barney, Gus and Dolly have all DEFINITELY gone before leaving. As I trudge home in the drizzly rain, all I can think is: this would NEVER have happened at my old school.

See, before I go any further, there's some stuff you should know. And the rest of this RIDONKULOUS story won't make sense without it, so don't go skipping to the next action-packed chapter, OK?

Pinky swear?

All right.

Until about two months ago, I was just a normal kid.

I lived by the sea, in Cornwall, in a little house next to the cafe my mum and dad ran. The cafe was called **Mr & Mrs Morris's Marvellous Munch Mansion.** ('If you think the name's a mouthful, wait till you see the size of our portions,' Mum used to say.) Anyway, trust me, it was the most AWESOME cafe ever! Dad did the cooking and Mum was the manager. I used to love being there on weekends, or after school, drawing my **ARLEY & TAPPER** cartoons while Dad whipped up crushed-almond-'n'-raspberry muffins or triple-choc gingerbread brownies, and Mum chatted with the customers.

Life was super-duper sweet.

Until everything changed. The cafe got sold, and Dad had to get a job at a yucktastic fast food restaurant called CHEEZY-DUZ-IT. Then they moved his job here to a tiny grey town near London – and now he and Mum are always too busy or stressed to even notice me.

The only thing we've got left to remind us of our cafe is the sign – a big glass 'M' that used to hang above the customers, and now just sits on our mantelpiece, looking lonely.

So, things at home are pretty gloomified. And school's not much better.

I've never been good at talking to people – my stupid face always goes red and the words get stuck in my throat. So after two months here I still haven't made one actual, proper friend. Most days, I just keep my head down and try to avoid being thumped by Barney Divney.

LIFE IS SUPER-DUPER UN-SWEET.

I guess that's why I've started drawing Arley and Tapper more and more. I don't mean to keep daydreaming and doodling – it's just that their world seems so much more colourful and FUN.

When I created Arley and Tapper, I gave them all the qualities I WISHED I had. Like, Arley is super brave and fearless. He can battle any bad guy and he'd never let ANYBODY thump him! And Tapper is silly and funny and makes everyone laugh, like I wish I could. They've each got their own special move too: Arley's high-flying **TAIL SPIN** and Tapper's bogey-blasting **SNOT SHOT**!

Just thinking about them makes me reach for my sketchbook. I've had it for years, this sketchbook – and you can really tell. It's all smushed round the edges because I carry it everywhere. Inside, it's full of **ARLEY & TAPPER** adventures, but on the back I've stuck loads of cool stickers of ZACK JELLICOE – the star of my favourite comic book series.

You've heard of him, right?

WHAT?! YOU HAVEN'T??

Where have you been living, in a Siberian CAVE?!

OK, so, in a nutshell: Zack Jellicoe is this teenage crime-fighting skateboarder. He's awesome.

He's drawn by Graham

'Yorky' York – the coolest cartoonist ever and my ULTIMATE hero. Yorky is usually described in magazines as being 'reclusive', which means you hardly ever see him. He lives in some remote part of Scotland where they probably don't even have Wi-Fi. Getting paid to sit on your own and draw cartoons all day – sounds like a dream come true.

He's only released three Zack Jellicoe comics: *Zack Jellicoe vs the BMX Burglar*, *Zack Jellicoe Meets the Scooter Squid Squad*, and *Zack Jellicoe and the Halfpipe of Doom*. I must've read them all about a zillion times. The last one came out FIVE YEARS ago, and I've been waiting and WAITING, but Yorky hasn't written a new one.

No idea why.

Anyway! Yorky's the COOLEST.

Once I even sent

him my three best **ARLEY & TAPPER** adventures to see what he thought:

1. **ARLEY & TAPPER** in the USA

2. **ARLEY & TAPPER**'s Mission to Mars

and

3. **ARLEY & TAPPER** vs the Six-Headed OctoShark

He hasn't written back yet, but I guess he's pretty busy.

I turn the corner on to my street, and the drizzle becomes full-on pouring rain. Even the WEATHER is against me today.

Suddenly I feel a painful YANK on my shoulder, and someone yells—

Yoink!

CHAPTER THREE

FART-MUNCH ATTACKS!

I spin round to see Barney Divney stood there, holding my rucksack like a trophy.

With him are his ghastly sidekicks (and 'sidekicks' really is the right word, as they mainly stand by his SIDE and KICK people).

'Hey!' I yell. I reach for my bag, but Gus and Dolly block me.

'Just wanted to see what the "great artist" has been drawing . . .' With a horrible grin, Barney pulls out my sketchbook and waves it about. 'Ah-ha!'

I feel panic wriggle right through me: 'Give it back! Please!'

But Barney just smirks an even smirkier smirk and opens my book. 'Oh my gosh . . . "Arley and Tapper",' he splutters. 'This is SO STUPID!'

Gus and Dolly start laughing. I'm still trying to grab my book, but I can feel my face getting hotter and hotter and my mouth getting drier and drier, and all that's running through my head is donotcrydonotcrydonotcryDONOTCRY.

Barney chucks the book to Gus. I run towards him, but Dolly sticks out a spidery hand to stop me. Gus starts thumbing through the pages with his grubby fingers.

'You're such a loser,' he barks. 'These are RUBBISH!' He looks up at Barney. 'Though this Fart-Munch guy does kind of look like you . . .'

'What?! No he DOESN'T!' Barney glares at me. 'I'll teach you to call ME Doctor Fart-Munch . . .'

'It's **PROFESSOR FART-MUNCH**,' Gus says.

'Whatever! Finn Morris can't draw to save his life!'

'That's not true!' I say, but I can hear the

wobble in my voice.

Dolly sneers down at me, wrinkling her stubby nose. 'Awwww, look! The little baby's going all red again now!'

They all start laughing harder. My face feels like it's literally ON FIRE. I can feel the tears starting to prickle in my eyes and I have to bite my lip to make them stop.

What would Arley and Tapper do? I wonder. They definitely wouldn't stand here looking like a wibbly little beetroot. No way. Tapper would smush Gus and Dolly with the **SNOT SHOT**! And Arley would thwack Barney with the **TAIL SPIN**!

But they're not here. They're not real. It's just me, on my own, like always.

Across the road, I see Isha Kapesa – the girl with the Avengers pencil case – walking past. She turns and looks at us, like she's about to say something. Like she's about to stick up for me. Barney shouts –

What you looking at, Kapesa?

She keeps walking.

I just want the ground to open up and swallow me. I want to disappear. Gus chucks my book back to Barney, who flicks to another page. He cackles. 'No wonder you don't have any friends. Who'd want to hang out with a red-faced baby who draws cartoons?!'

I try to speak, but the lump in my throat won't let me. And, anyway – maybe Barney is right. Everyone in class was laughing at me too.

They must all think I'm a loser.

'OK, this is boring now,' Dolly yawns. 'Barney, give Baby Red-Face his book back, and let's go.'

Barney dangles the book towards me. 'All right. Here . . . FETCH!'

He tosses my sketchbook like a Frisbee into a wet hedge.

Gus and Dolly burst into horrible hysterics and I watch the rain soak into the pages, spoiling the **ARLEY & TAPPER** strips I've spent months – years – drawing.

Barney leans in so close I can smell his cheese-and-oniony breath. He whispers, 'Don't worry – your drawings are rubbish anyway.'

Then the three of them gallop away, cackling like horrid hyenas. And now that I'm finally alone, I un-bite my lip and let the tears come.

CHAPTER FOUR

A BIG FAT FAIRY TALE

I slump home in the rain, feeling more awful than I've ever felt.

I can feel my sketchbook bumping against my back through my rucksack. I'd rescued it from the soggy hedge, but right now I'm not even sure why I bothered.

I watch the water streaming into the metal drains at the side of the road, and it's like I can see everything else slithering down there with it.

All my life I've had this dream that I'll be a famous cartoonist one day – that **ARLEY & TAPPER** will be loved all over the world, like The Simpsons or The Avengers or Zack Jellicoe.

And now I can see that dream for what it really is: just a big fat fairy tale.

I'm not a 'great artist'. I'm just a loser doodler with no friends.

I'm nobody.

*

During dinner, Mum and Dad barely even notice me.

Back in Cornwall, dinner time was the BESTEST time. After Mum and Dad closed the cafe, we'd sit around the table, laughing and telling each other about our days. Even though Dad had been cooking all day, he'd still knock up something amazing to eat – his famous fricasséed fishcakes or his legendary lamb lasagne – and Mum had a tradition where we all had to say ONE NEW THING we'd learnt that day. It could be anything, no matter how random or silly. Like maybe . . .

Dad: **I learnt a shrimp's heart is in its head!**

Mum: **I learnt the queen is a trained car mechanic!**

Finn: **I learnt I can fit three whole fingers into my left nostril!**

Mum and Dad: **Ewwww!!! Finn!**

But that tradition has been totally forgotten now. Dad just sits there looking tired in his CHEEZY-DUZ-IT work shirt, pushing the sludgy lentil curry he's microwaved for us around his plate. Mum just mumbles gloomily about how WORRIED she is that she can't find a new job. The only time they even speak to me is when Mum nudges my elbow and mutters, 'Clean plate please, Pooka.'

('Pooka' is what my mum calls me sometimes. DON'T LAUGH. I bet YOUR mum's got a silly name for YOU too.)

After I've helped wash up, I go to my room. I take out my damp sketchbook and turn to the comic I was working on in maths. Arley and Tapper are still dangling there, off the edge of the bridge, ready to pull up the bus full of kittens and save the day. There's only one frame left to draw. It feels . . . wrong to leave it empty. I've never, EVER, left an **ARLEY & TAPPER** adventure unfinished.

But I just don't feel like drawing them any more.

I hear a scratching at the door, and Milligan slinks in and hops up on to my desk. I stroke him behind his ears and mutter: 'Oh, Milligan, what am I gonna do, man?'

He purrs back as if to say: 'I'm a cat, mate, don't ask me.'

I flick through the wet, blotchy sketchbook and I can still hear Gus and Dolly's jeering laughter as Barney called me a red-faced little baby. I can still smell his horrid breath as he whispered, 'Your drawings are RUBBISH anyway.'

And he's right.

Yorky didn't even write back when I sent them to him. He must have thought they were stupid too.

I feel the tears start to prickle again as a cold, hard thought forms clearly inside my head:

I'm going to stop drawing cartoons.

Outside, the rain batters on the window. I pick up my sketchbook and drop it into the wastepaper bin, with all the other rubbish.

Milligan starts purring and bumping his furry head against the bin, like he's trying to knock it over. Like he's trying to rescue my stupid book.

'Come here, you silly cat.' I pick him up, but he wriggles free and goes back to bumping the bin.

'Suit yourself,' I sigh.

And then I climb into bed and try to sleep.

CHAPTER FIVE

WHAT WOULD ARLEY AND TAPPER DO?

Something's wrong. That's the first thing I think as I wake up in the morning with a start, my eyes all crunkled with sleep gunk.

I can't put my finger on exactly what is wrong. But I somehow know for SURE that something WEIRD is going on.

Ah, hang on. That's what it is: I can hear whispering. Little scratchy voices, all around my head.

This happens a lot. The walls in this house are

pretty thin, and Mum and Dad sometimes go to sleep listening to the radio, which is usually still playing in the morning.

I put my fist up to give the wall a THWACK, when I notice something else.

Something MUCH MORE SCARY.

There's someone in the room with me.

Through the darkness, I can see two big, blurry shapes by the door. I can't make out who – or what – they are. But they're WAY bigger than Milligan. They're . . .

Hang on.

They're the ones whispering.

I'm WIDE AWAKE now, my tummy swirling like it's full of angry snakes.

I feel my face go full-blown beetroot. Every bone in my body is tingling with terror.

WHO ARE THEY?!

Are they BURGLARS? Burglars don't break into your house and then just sit there mumbling, do they?!

OH, MONKEY NUTS . . .

My mouth is so dry I can barely BREATHE. But what am I supposed to do? I can't stay wrapped up in my duvet for ever, can I?

'Come on, Finn,' I tell myself. 'Pull yourself together. What would Arley and Tapper do?'

I gulp some air and get ready to scream for my parents or the police or ANYONE . . .

And then I switch on the light.

But when I see them, I can't scream.

I can't move. I can't do anything.

Because at the other end of the room . . .

ARLEY AND TAPPER ARE STARING STRAIGHT BACK AT ME!

CHAPTER SIX

WHUUUUUUUUUUUUUUU?!!!!

My head feels like it's been shoved in a top-speed tumble dryer.

My eyes feel like they've been pulled out and put back in upside down.

My brain feels like it's been chucked in a blender and made into a delicious, nutritious **BRAIN SMOOTHIE.**

I try to speak – to shout for help – but all that comes out is:

'Whuuuuuuuuuuuuuu?!!!!'

'Who are you?' says Arley. 'Are you the bad guy? Is this your villainous lair? Tell us right now, matey-chops, or I'm gonna hit you with a TAIL SPIN so fast you'll think you're doing the tango with a tornado!'

Tapper leaps up on to the bed, his giant nose wobbling like a jellied cucumber. 'Yeah! And I've got a bose full of nogies with your name on it!'

Arley rolls his eyes. 'Ignore my friend here. He's got the IQ of a Honey Nut Loop.'

What in the sweet, sweet name of **MONKEY NUTS** is going on???

I MUST be dreaming.

It's just a super-duper-scarily-realistic dream in which two **ACTUAL, FULL-SIZE CARTOON CHARACTERS** have come to life. **ACTUAL, FULL-SIZE CARTOON CHARACTERS** that I created.

I shut my eyes tight, to try and make the nightmare stop. But when I open them again, Arley and Tapper are still there, standing over me.

I try again to speak, but all that comes out is:

'Bhuuuuuuuuuuu'

'D'you reckon he's really the bad guy?' Tapper says. **'He's not very scary, is he?'**

Arley frowns. **'Think you're right, Taps – he's hiding under a duvet for starters. Look matey-boy, are you the villain or not?'**

'Nuuuhhh'

I groan.

Arley puffs out his cheeks. **'Well, that's a relief. I was worried the standard of villains had seriously dropped.'**

They both flop down and sit on the bed either side of me.

I can't believe what I'm seeing. I've only ever

drawn Arley and Tapper flat, in two dimensions, and now they're here – in three dimensions, in front of me. I also can't believe I'm hearing their voices. Voices that, actually, sound a bit like mine. But it's the silly, cartoony versions of my voice I use when I'm writing their dialogue in my head.

'And who's this wickle guy?!' Tapper squeals and scoops Milligan up off the floor. **'You're not the bad guy, are you? No, you're way too CUTE to be the bad guy! Who's a wickle cutesy-wutesy?!!'**

He starts tickling Milligan with his giant nose. Milligan seems to like it.

I finally manage to find some proper words. 'You're . . . Are you really . . .

Arley and Tapper?'

I croak.

Arley grins. **'You've heard of us, eh? Doesn't surprise me. We're a pretty big deal. We've saved the world, like, twenty trillion times. Anyway, who are YOU?'**

'F-F-Finn Morris,' I stutter.

'OK, F-F-Finn Morris, tell me: where the f-f-flip are we?'

'In . . . my bedroom.'

'And when exactly is the adventure gonna start?'

'The what?'

'You know: the adventure,' Arley snaps. 'Every day, me and Tapper have an adventure. We find ourselves in some totally random place, some wacky stuff happens, we fight a bad guy and we save the day.'

'It's sort of our whole thing,' Tapper grins.

I open my mouth to speak, even though I have literally NO CLUE what to say.

But before I can make a sound, there's a knock on the bedroom door.

'Finn?' I hear my dad whisper. 'What's going on in there?'

CHAPTER SEVEN

OLD SOCKS AND CAT FARTS

'OH, **MONKEY NUTS!**' I hiss.

'Who's that?' Arley jumps into karate pose.

'THAT must be the bad guy!' Tapper leaps up from the bed. **'And I've got a BOSE full of NOGIES with his . . . OH, MONKEY NUTS. I've done it AGAIN!'** He slaps a finger to his giant nose: **'Anyway, here comes the . . . SNOT SHOT!'**

'NO!!!' I jump forward to block the flying bogies . . . But none come out.

'Hm.' Tapper flicks his nose. **'That was weird. Why didn't it work?'**

There's another knock on the door. Without thinking, I grab Arley and Tapper and drag them towards my wardrobe.

'Oi!' shouts Arley. **'Unhand us!'**

I still don't know WHAT is going on, but I do know that the situation won't be helped by a real-life cartoon character **SNOT SHOTTING** my dad.

'Just stay in here till he's gone, and please be quiet!' I beg.

'Is this part of the adventure?' Arley demands.

'What? I don't know? Yes! Just stay in there!'

They roll their eyes and step back into the wardrobe as I close the door. At the EXACT moment it clicks shut, my dad pokes his head into the room.

'Finnbar? Everything OK in here?'

'Yup,' I squeak, even though everything in here is about as un-OK as it's possible to be.

Dad's already got his CHEEZY-DUZ-IT uniform on, and he looks as gloomified as ever. 'I thought I heard you talking to someone?'

'Er . . . nope.'

There's a muffled THWUNK! from inside the wardrobe. My heart jumps up into my throat.

'What was that?' Dad asks.

'Er . . . that was, erm, Milligan,' I stammer. I can see Milligan quite clearly, curled up under my desk, thankfully out of Dad's sight.

Dad narrows his eyes. 'You shouldn't shut the cat in the wardrobe, Finn.'

'No, I know. I just thought he . . . might want some privacy. I'll let him out now.'

Dad makes the face of a man who thinks his son has COMPLETELY and UTTERLY lost it. Which is fair enough, because maybe I have.

'R-i-i-ight . . .' he says slowly. 'Anyway, breakfast is ready, so . . .'

I nod, feeling my stomach whooooosh horribly as Milligan starts to stroll out from under the desk . . .

'I'll be right down,' I gulp.

Dad gives the wardrobe one more look and then leaves, stepping STRAIGHT over Milligan without noticing him!

As I breathe out in ALMIGHTY relief, the wardrobe bursts open and Arley and Tapper come tumbling out.

Tapper pinches his nose and says, **'Yeeeesh! I thought he was never gonna leave. It smells like old socks and cat farts in there!'**

Arley flops on to my bed. **'Listen, Finn Morris. Bit of advice: in future, it's probably best if you don't stuff us in a wardrobe when the action starts. We can't exactly have an adventure inside a cat-fart cupboard, can we?'**

'This is NOT an adventure!' I whisper-yell. 'This is a . . . dream! Or a nightmare! Or . . . I don't know WHAT this is! I mean . . . Where did you two even come from?!'

Tapper shrugs. **'From Toon World, obvs.'**

'Toon World?! Where's that?!'

'Dunno.' He scratches his fox ears. **'I was never much cop at geography. But Toon World's where we live. It's a RIDONKULOUSLY awesome place! It's where our adventures happen.'**

'Yes, but it was the STRANGEST thing, actually,' Arley says. 'We were in the middle of our latest adventure – we'd just defeated the evil PROFESSOR FART-MUNCH, and we were hanging off this bridge, trying to save a bus full of kittens—'

Tapper raises his finger. 'Adorable kittens!'

Arley rolls his eyes. 'Yes, Taps, adorable kittens. Anyway, it felt like we'd been hanging there FOR EVER. Normally our adventures . . . end. We save the day, and then we move on to the next one. But this time . . . we just kept hanging there and hanging there and hanging there.'

'My arms were KILLING me,' Tapper groans.

'And then, finally . . . everything just went black,' Arley says.

'Next thing we knew, we woke up in YOUR bedroom, Finnster,' says Tapper. 'So if anyone owes anyone an explanation, it's YOU.'

I try to wrap my brain around what's happening, but I just CAN'T. My mind is fizzing and spluttering like a busted microwave. There's a shout from downstairs. 'FINN!' Mum yells. 'YOUR BOILED EGGS ARE GETTING COLD!'

Tapper smacks his lips together. **'Ooh, I flippin' LOVE beiled oggs! No, wait, I mean . . .'**

Mum will be stomping upstairs within seconds if I don't get moving. 'I need to go down to breakfast,' I say. 'Please stay here and try to be quiet. I'll be back up in a sec and we'll figure out what to do.'

'Bring back some oiled beggs!' Tapper shouts, as I slam the door behind me.

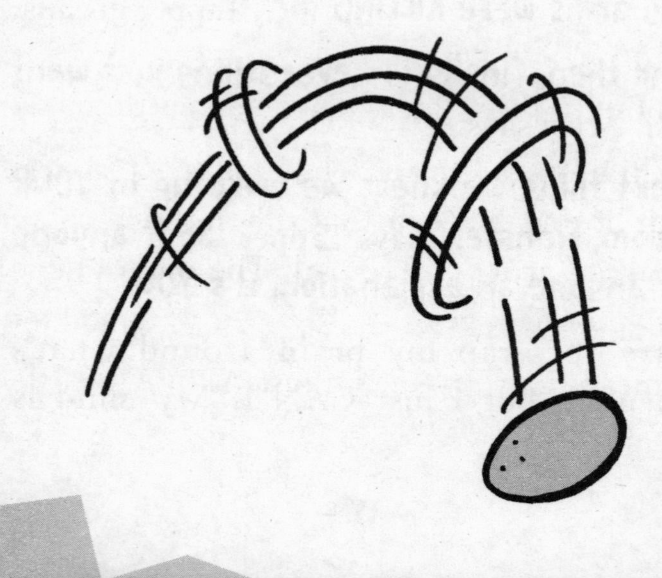

CHAPTER EIGHT

BIT OVERCOOKED

All through breakfast, I'm actually GLAD that Mum and Dad barely seem to notice I'm there. Otherwise they would spot that:

1) I'm not eating.

2) I'm not drinking.

3) I'm shaking like a jelly in an earthquake.

While they crunch their toast and talk about boring work stuff, a zillion thoughts are pinballing around my head. The main one is, *How did this happen?!*

I mean, cartoons don't just APPEAR in the

real world, do they?? And if they do . . . how do you send them back??

Dad sighs as he scoops gloopy egg on to his burnt toast. 'I've got more training at work today. They're teaching us how to cook battered sausages in fried cheese.' He shakes his head sadly. 'When I think of the amazing stuff I used to cook at our cafe . . .'

'It'll get better, love,' says Mum, though she doesn't sound very convinced. 'Anyway, at least you've got a job. I'm still down at the Jobcentre every day. And the bills are piling up . . .'

They carry on mumbling gloomily as I excuse myself from the table. They don't notice me sneaking two boiled eggs into my pockets, and waddling out of the room like a duck that needs a wee.

(Don't laugh! I'm trying not to crack them inside my PJs.)

When I get upstairs, I stand outside my bedroom door for a second and take a deep breath. Because maybe . . . maybe I've just imagined this whole thing. Yeah! Of course I have! Nothing this BANANAS could actually happen in real life!

But . . . no.

I push the door open and there's Arley, lying sprawled out on my bed, while Tapper sits at my desk, twitching his fox ears at Milligan. Milligan is twitching his cat ears right back.

'What's the egg situation, Finnbot?' Tapper asks.

I chuck him a boiled egg, and he drops it straight into his mouth with the shell still on.

'Bit overcooked,' he grumbles.

'Look, we need to figure out what we're gonna do,' I say. 'Because I've got to go to school now.'

'Great!' Arley stands up. **'We'll come too.'**

'No way!' I hiss. 'If anyone sees you, they'll totally freak out!'

'Rude,' says Tapper, making a face.

'Sorry, that came out wrong,' I explain. 'It's just that people around here aren't used to seeing

CARTOONS walking around. Especially ones with massive noses and fox ears and floppy tails! If anyone saw you they'd want to . . . put you in a museum, or a science lab, or something.'

'Well, we're not staying here,' huffs Arley, glaring around my bedroom. **'This is the most boring adventure we've ever had so far. Eating eggs and hiding in cat-farty cupboards – woop-di-flippin'-doo.'**

I put my head in my hands and mutter, **'OH, MONKEY NUTS!'**

'And that's another thing,' Arley snaps. **'Stop saying "monkey nuts"! "Monkey nuts" is TAPPER's catchphrase.'**

'Yeah, dude,' Tapper sniffs. **'Don't make me get the lawyers involved.'**

I stare at him. This is too, too FREAKY. They don't realize that I created them. I came up with all their catchphrases and adventures and everything about them!

But there's no time to think about that. The only thing that matters right now is making sure they both stay hidden while I'm at school. Then, when I get back, I can try to figure out a plan. So, maybe . . . maybe, if they think they're on another adventure, then the best thing is just to play along . . .

'OK, look . . .' I say. 'If I tell you about the adventure – the REAL adventure – will you promise to stay hidden until I get back?'

Arley crosses his arms. **'Keep talking, Finn Morris . . .'**

'OK, the plan is . . .' I start pulling words at random from my frazzled brain. 'The plan is that . . . when I come back from school . . . you're going to fight **PROFESSOR FART-MUNCH!**'

Arley slams his fist into his hand. **'Fart-Munch! I should have known that dastardly dimwit would be back to seek his revenge! Well, we'll be ready for him!'**

Tapper spins round and round in my chair. **'Hoooo, Mama – I am gonna be SNOT SHOTTING tonight!'**

'Yes, yes,' I nod. 'You're going to defeat the bad guy and save the day, like always. But first you HAVE to stay here until I get back! If anyone sees you . . . the adventure's over! Got it?'

Arley winks at me. **'A top-secret mission, eh? You want us to keep our identities hidden?'**

'Exactly!'

I hear my mum stomping up the stairs, yelling, 'FINN! TIME FOR SCHOOL!'

'I need to go,' I hiss. 'Just promise you'll stay hidden until you hear us leave. And then stay in the house, and don't cause any trouble. Got it?'

Tapper stands up and salutes me, like an army officer. **'You can trust us, Finntasmo! We don't even know the MEANING of the word**

CHAPTER NINE

AT HOME WITH ARLEY AND TAPPER

Dressing up in Finn's mum's clothes
Dressing up Milligan in Finn's mum and dad's clothes
Having a MAHOOSIVE pillow fight
(while eating three packs of dark chocolate digestives)
A

Having a sword fight with a baguette
En garde, Sir
Tapper could do with a helm
This fits perfectly
Finn's book falls out of the bin
FINN MORRIS

Hmmm —
what's this?
FINN MORRIS
Why has the Finnster got pictures of US, Arl? Is he a spy or something?
FINN MORRIS
I don't know Taps —
but we're gonna FIND OUT!

FIND OUT WHAT HAPPENS NEXT!

Get the book!
TOM ELLEN
PHIL CORBETT
THE CARTOONS THAT CAME TO LIFE